Dear Carys Happy 7th Birthday

lots of love Grandma & Alan

xx

THE RAILWAY SERIES
TROUBLESOME ENGINES

by
THE REV. W. AWDRY

with illustrations by
C. REGINALD DALBY

EGMONT

EGMONT

We bring stories to life

First published in 1950
This edition published in 2015
by Egmont UK Limited
The Yellow Building, 1 Nicholas Road, London W11 4AN

Thomas the Tank Engine & Friends ™

CREATED BY BRITT ALLCROFT

Based on the Railway Series by the Reverend W Awdry
© 2015 Gullane (Thomas) LLC. Thomas the Tank Engine & Friends and
Thomas & Friends are trademarks of Gullane (Thomas) Limited.
Thomas the Tank Engine & Friends and Design is Reg. U.S. Pat. & Tm. Off.
© 2015 HIT Entertainment Limited.

HiT entertainment

ISBN 978 1 4052 7653 5
59718/1
Printed in Malaysia

DEAR FRIENDS,

News from the Line has not been good. The Fat Controller has been having trouble. A short while ago he gave Henry a coat of green paint; but as soon as he got his old colour back again, Henry became conceited. Gordon and James, too, have been Getting Above Themselves.

I am glad to say, however, that The Fat Controller has, quite kindly but very firmly, put them In Their Place; and the trains are running as usual.

I hope you will like meeting Percy; we shall be hearing more of him later.

THE AUTHOR

HENRY AND THE ELEPHANT

HENRY and Gordon were lonely when Thomas left the Yard to run his Branch Line. They missed him very much.

They had more work to do. They couldn't wait in the Shed till it was time, and find their coaches at the platform; they had to fetch them. They didn't like that.

Edward sometimes did odd jobs, and so did James, but James soon started grumbling too. The Fat Controller kindly gave Henry and Gordon new coats of paint (Henry chose green), but they still grumbled dreadfully.

"We get no rest, we get no rest," they complained as they clanked about the Yard; but the coaches only laughed.

"You're lazy and slack, you're lazy and slack," they answered in their quiet, rude way.

But when a Circus came to town, the engines forgot they were tired. They all wanted to shunt the special trucks and coaches.

They were dreadfully jealous of James when The Fat Controller told him to pull the train when the Circus went away.

However, they soon forgot about the animals as they had plenty of work to do.

One morning Henry was told to take some workmen to a tunnel which was blocked.

He grumbled away to find two trucks to carry the workmen and their tools.

"Pushing trucks! Pushing trucks!" he muttered in a sulky sort of way.

They stopped outside the tunnel, and tried to look through it, but it was quite dark; no daylight shone from the other end.

The workmen took their tools and went inside.

Suddenly with a shout they all ran out looking frightened.

"We went to the block and started to dig, but it grunted and moved," they said.

"Rubbish," said the Foreman.

"It's not rubbish, it's big and alive; we're not going in there again."

"Right," said the Foreman, "I'll ride in a truck and Henry shall push it out."

"Wheeeesh," said Henry unhappily. He hated tunnels (he had been shut up in one once), but this was worse; something big and alive was inside.

"Peep peep peep pip pip pee—eep!" he whistled, "I don't want to go in!"

"Neither do I," said his Driver, "but we must clear the line."

"Oh dear! Oh dear!" puffed Henry as they slowly advanced into the darkness.

B U M P ———!!!!

Henry's Driver shut off steam at once.

"Help! Help! we're going back," wailed Henry, and slowly moving out into the daylight came first Henry, then the trucks, and last of all, pushing hard and rather cross, came a large elephant.

"Well I never did!" said the Foreman. "It's an elephant from the Circus."

Henry's Driver put on his brakes, and a man ran to telephone for the Keeper.

The elephant stopped pushing and came towards them. They gave him some sandwiches and cake, so he forgot he was cross and remembered he was hungry. He drank three buckets of water without stopping, and was just going to drink another when Henry let off steam.

The elephant jumped, and "hoo——oosh", he squirted the water over Henry by mistake.

Poor Henry!

When the Keeper came, the workmen rode home happily in the trucks, laughing at their adventure, but Henry was very cross.

"An elephant pushed me! an elephant hooshed me!" he hissed.

He was sulky all day, and his coaches had an uncomfortable time.

In the Shed he told Gordon and James about the elephant, and I am sorry to say that instead of laughing and telling him not to be silly, they looked sad and said:

"You poor engine, you have been badly treated."

TENDERS AND TURNTABLES

THE big stations at both ends of the line each have a turntable. The Fat Controller had them made so that Edward, Henry, Gordon and James can be turned round. It is dangerous for Tender Engines to go fast backwards. Tank Engines like Thomas don't need turntables; they can go just as well backwards as forwards.

But if you had heard Gordon talking a short while ago, you would have thought that The Fat Controller had given him a tender just to show how important he was.

"You don't understand, little Thomas," said Gordon, "we Tender Engines have a position to keep up. You haven't a tender and that makes a difference. It doesn't matter where *you* go, but We are Important, and for The Fat Controller to make us shunt trucks, fetch coaches, and go on some of those dirty sidings it's — it's — well it's not the Proper Thing."

And Gordon puffed away in a dignified manner.

Thomas chuckled and went off with Annie and Clarabel.

Arrived at the Terminus, Gordon waited till all the passengers had got out; then, groaning and grumbling, he shunted the coaches to another platform.

"Disgraceful! Disgraceful!" he hissed as he ran backwards to the turntable.

The turntable was in a windy place close to the sea. It was only just big enough for Gordon, and if he was not on it just right, he put it out of balance, and made it difficult to turn.

Today, Gordon was in a bad temper, and the wind was blowing fiercely.

His Driver tried to make him stop in the right place; backwards and forwards they went, but Gordon wasn't trying.

At last Gordon's Driver gave it up. The Fireman tried to turn the handle, but Gordon's weight and the strong wind prevented him. The Driver, some Platelayers, and the Fireman all tried together.

"It's no good," they said at last, mopping their faces, "your tender upsets the balance. If you were a nice Tank Engine, you'd be all right. Now you'll have to pull the next train backwards."

Gordon came to the platform. Some little boys shouted, "Come on quick, here's a new Tank Engine."

"What a swiz!" they said, when they came near, "it's only Gordon, back to front."

Gordon hissed emotionally.

He puffed to the Junction. "Hullo!" called Thomas, "playing Tank Engines? Sensible engine! Take my advice, scrap your tender and have a nice bunker instead."

Gordon snorted, but didn't answer. Even James laughed when he saw him. "Take care," hissed Gordon, "you might stick too."

"No fear," chuckled James, "I'm not so fat as you."

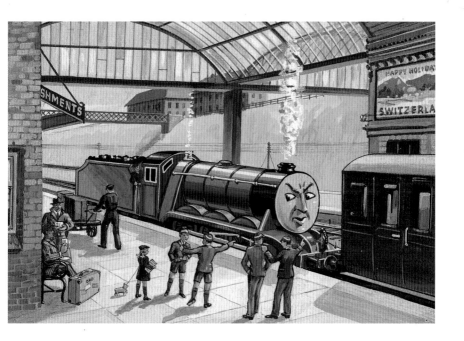

"I mustn't stick," thought James anxiously, as he ran to the turntable later. He stopped on just the right place to balance the table. It could now swing easily. His Fireman turned the handle . . . James turned . . . much too easily! The wind puffed him round like a top. He couldn't stop! . . .

At last the wind died down, and James stopped turning, but not before Gordon, who had been turned on the loop line, had seen him.

"Well! Well!" he said, "are you playing roundabouts?"

Poor James, feeling quite giddy, rolled off to the Shed without a word.

That night the three engines had an "indignation meeting".

"It's shameful to treat Tender Engines like this! Henry gets 'hooshed' by elephants; Gordon has to go backwards and people think he's a Tank Engine. James spins round like a top, and everyone laughs at us. And added to that, The Fat Controller makes us shunt in dirty sidings. Ugh ——!!" said all three engines together.

"Listen," said Gordon . . . He whispered something to the others: "We'll do it tomorrow. The Fat Controller *will* look silly!"

TROUBLE IN THE SHED

THE Fat Controller sat in his office and listened. The Fat Controller frowned and said, "What a nuisance passengers are! How can I work with all this noise?"

The Stationmaster knocked and came in, looking worried.

"There's trouble in the Shed, Sir. Henry is sulking; there is no train, and the passengers are saying this is a Bad Railway."

"Indeed!" said The Fat Controller. "We cannot allow that. Will you quieten the passengers, please; I will go and speak to Henry."

He found Henry, Gordon and James looking sulky.

"Come along, Henry," he said, "it is time your train was ready."

"Henry's not going," said Gordon rudely. "We *won't* shunt like Common Tank Engines. We are Important Tender Engines. You fetch our coaches and we will pull them. Tender Engines don't shunt," and all three engines let off steam in a cheeky way.

"Oh indeed," said The Fat Controller severely. "We'll see about that; engines on My Railway do as they are told."

He hurried away, climbed into his car and drove to find Edward.

"The Yard has never been the same since Thomas left," he thought sadly.

Edward was shunting.

"Leave those trucks please, Edward; I want you to push coaches for me in the Yard."

"Thank you, Sir, that will be a nice change."

"That's a good engine," said The Fat Controller kindly, "off you go then."

So Edward found coaches for the three engines, and that day the trains ran as usual.

But when The Fat Controller came next morning, Edward looked unhappy.

Gordon came clanking past, hissing rudely. "Bless me!" said The Fat Controller. "What a noise!"

"They all hiss me, Sir," answered Edward sadly. "They say 'Tender Engines don't shunt', and last night they said I had black wheels. I haven't, have I, Sir?"

"No, Edward, you have nice blue ones, and I'm proud of you. Tender Engines do shunt, but all the same you'd be happier in your own Yard. We need a Tank Engine here."

He went to an Engine Workshop, and they showed him all sorts of Tank Engines. There were big ones, and little ones; some looked happy, and some sad, and some looked at him anxiously, hoping he would choose them.

At last he saw a smart little green engine with four wheels.

"That's the one," he thought.

"If I choose you, will you work hard?"

"Oh Sir! Yes Sir!"

"That's a good engine; I'll call you Percy."

"Yes Sir! Thank you Sir!" said Percy happily.

So he bought Percy and drove him back to the Yard.

"Edward," he called, "here's Percy; will you show him everything?"

Percy soon learned what he had to do, and they had a happy afternoon.

Once Henry came by hissing as usual.

"Whee —— eesh!" said Percy suddenly; Henry jumped and ran back to the Shed.

"How beautifully you wheeshed him," laughed Edward. "I can't wheesh like that."

"Oh!" said Percy modestly, "that's nothing; you should hear them in the workshop. You have to wheesh loudly to make yourself heard."

Next morning Thomas arrived. "The Fat Controller sent for me; I expect he wants help," he said importantly to Edward.

"Sh! Sh! here he comes."

"Well done Thomas; you've been quick. Listen, Henry, Gordon and James are sulking; they say they won't shunt like Common Tank Engines. So I have shut them up, and I want you both to run the line."

"Common Tank Engines indeed!" snorted Thomas. "We'll show them."

"And Percy here will help too," said The Fat Controller.

"Oh Sir! Yes Sir! Please Sir!" answered Percy excitedly.

Edward and Thomas worked the line. Starting at opposite ends, they pulled the trains, whistling cheerfully to each other as they passed.

Percy sometimes puffed along the Branch Line. Thomas was anxious, but both Driver and Guard promised to take care of Annie and Clarabel.

There were fewer trains, but the passengers didn't mind; they knew the three other engines were having a Lesson.

Henry, Gordon and James stayed shut in the Shed, and were cold, lonely and miserable. They wished now they hadn't been so silly.

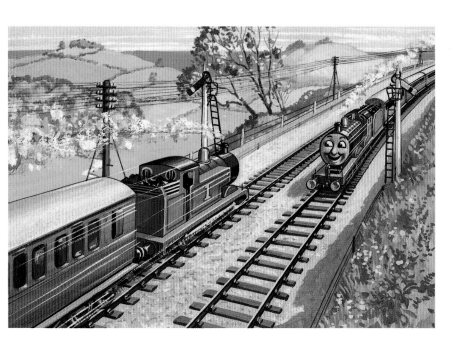

PERCY RUNS AWAY

HENRY, Gordon and James were shut up for several days. At last The Fat Controller opened the Shed.

"I hope you are sorry," he said sternly, "and understand you are not so important after all. Thomas, Edward and Percy have worked the line very nicely. They need a change, and I will let you out if you promise to be good."

"Yes Sir!" said the three engines, "we will."

"That's right, but please remember that this 'no shunting' nonsense must stop."

He told Edward, Thomas and Percy that they could go and play on the Branch Line for a few days.

They ran off happily and found Annie and Clarabel at the Junction. The two coaches were so pleased to see Thomas again, and he took them for a run at once. Edward and Percy played with trucks.

"Stop! Stop! Stop!" screamed the trucks as they were pushed into their proper sidings, but the two engines laughed and went on shunting till the trucks were tidily arranged.

Next, Edward took some empty trucks to the Quarry, and Percy was left alone.

Percy didn't mind that a bit; he liked watching trains and being cheeky to the engines.

"Hurry! Hurry! Hurry!" he would call to them. Gordon, Henry and James got very cross!

After a while he took some trucks over the Main Line to another siding. When they were tidy, he ran on to the Main Line again, and waited for the Signalman to set the points so that he could cross back to the Yard.

Edward had warned Percy: "Be careful on the Main Line; whistle to tell the Signalman you are there."

But Percy didn't remember to whistle, and the Signalman was so busy, and forgot Percy.

Bells rang in the signal box; the man answered, saying the line was clear, and set the signals for the next train.

Percy waited and waited; the points were still against him. He looked along the Main Line . . . "Peep! Peep!" he whistled in horror for, rushing straight towards him, was Gordon with the Express.

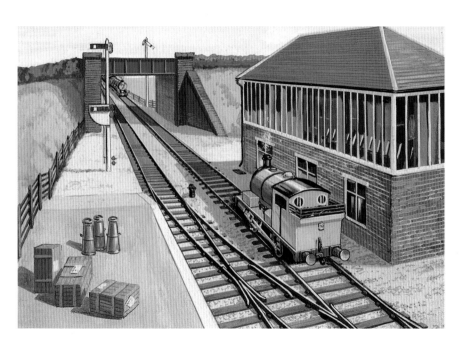

"Poop poop poo-poo-poop!" whistled Gordon. His Driver shut off steam and applied the brakes.

Percy's Driver turned on full steam. "Back Percy! Back!" he urged; but Percy's wheels wouldn't turn quickly. Gordon was coming so fast that it seemed he couldn't stop. With shut eyes Percy waited for the crash. His Driver and Fireman jumped out.

"Oo —— ooh e —— er!" groaned Gordon. "Get out of my way."

Percy opened his eyes; Gordon had stopped with Percy's buffers a few inches from his own.

But Percy had begun to move. "I — won't stay — here — I'll — run — a — way," he puffed. He was soon clear of the station and running as fast as he could. He went through Edward's station whistling loudly, and was so frightened that he ran right up Gordon's hill without stopping.

He was tired then, and wanted to stop, but he couldn't . . . he had no Driver to shut off steam and to apply the brakes.

"I shall have to run till my wheels wear out," he thought sadly. "Oh dear! Oh dear!"

"I — want — to — stop, I — want — to — stop," he puffed in a tired sort of way.

He passed another signal box. "I know just what you want, little Percy," called the man kindly. He set the points, and Percy puffed wearily on to a nice empty siding ending in a big bank of earth.

Percy was too tired now to care where he went. "I — want — to — stop, I — want — to — stop ——— I — *have* — stopped!" he puffed thankfully, as his bunker buried itself in the bank.

"Never mind, Percy," said the workmen as they dug him out, "you shall have a drink and some coal, and then you'll feel better."

Presently Gordon arrived.

"Well done, Percy, you started so quickly that you stopped a nasty accident."

"I'm sorry I was cheeky," said Percy, "you were clever to stop."

Percy now works in the Yard and finds coaches for the trains. He is still cheeky because he is that sort of engine, but he is always *most* careful when he goes on the Main Line.

Collect more stories about Thomas and his friends!

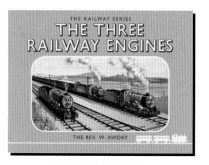

ISBN 9781405276498

ISBN 9781405276511

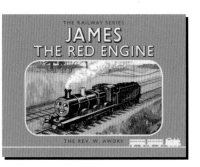

ISBN 9781405276504

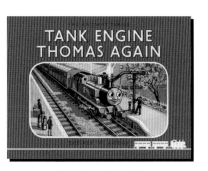

ISBN 9781405276528